God Is My Friend

A Kid's Guide to God

Written by
Lisa O. Engelhardt

Illustrated by
R. W. Alley

ONE
CARING
PLACE

Abbey Press
St. Meinrad, IN 47577

For my friend Patrice,
whose spirit, wisdom, sense of fun,
and genuine goodness
have given me so many glimpses of God
through the years.

Text © 2002 Lisa O. Engelhardt
Illustrations © 2002 St. Meinrad Archabbey
Published by One Caring Place
Abbey Press
St. Meinrad, Indiana 47577

Library of Congress Catalog Number
2001097959

ISBN 0-87029-361-3

Printed in the United States of America

A Message to Parents, Teachers, and Other Caring Adults

One night, as we were saying bedtime prayers, my daughter asked, "What good does it do to pray anyway? Aren't we all just in God's video game?" Her five-year-old imagination had conjured up a God who yanks us around in the game of life with a giant joystick. This was not the image of God I wanted to pass on to my children! How do we help children to get close to God—to see God as a loving, understanding, helpful Friend?

Children four to six are highly susceptible either to benevolent images of a loving God or to frightening images of God as a powerful avenger. Try to steer impressionable minds to a God who is a gentle, caring Friend. Small children can readily relate to a God who is as warm and snuggly as a teddy bear, or a God who watches over them as a mother bird cares for her hatchlings. Knowing that God is with them everyday, everywhere, helps to ease the fear of abandonment that many children of this age experience.

Seven- to nine-year-olds approach life more logically and want the real lowdown on God. You can point out that we come to know God by the marvelous things God has made and done. From atoms to galaxies, from dew-strung cobwebs to canyon vistas, God's "fingerprints" are everywhere. Yet God is more than just a remote Creator-Operator of the World. God is our personal Friend. Because children of this age are becoming more socially aware, they will readily understand the implications of sharing such a close relationship with God.

Talk with your children about how God has been a Friend in your own life. Let them see you spend time with your Friend in prayer, and talk about why and how you pray. Show them how to engage in "conversational" prayer—informal, sincere, and trusting dialogue with a God who listens and cares.

As you and your children read this book and grow closer to God, may you find comfort and love in the warm embrace of your Best Friend.

—Lisa O. Engelhardt

Your Best Friend

If you had a computer program to create a "Best Friend," what would this friend be like? Which of the choices below would you click on?

caring	happy	kind
honest	fun	helpful
likes the same	loving	good listener
stuff I do	interesting	awesome

God is all of this and much, much more. God is the very Best Friend a kid could ever have!

You Can Be Yourself

With a true friend, you feel free to be yourself. It's the same way with God. You don't have to "put on an act" for God to like you. To God, you already are a star!

If you're not any good at playing dodge ball, that's okay with God. If you think you have too many freckles, don't worry. God thinks you look just fine. If you're in a bad mood sometimes, God can take it.

Do your best to be yourself, and you'll always be good enough for God.

A Friend Likes to Be With You

A little puppy dog wiggles and waggles all over when her owner comes home. She is *so* glad to see the person she loves.

God feels that way about you—times a zillion! You make God happy just because you're YOU! God loves to see you and spend time with you.

Sometimes, if you just sit still with your eyes closed and think about God, you can feel God smiling back at you. Being with your Best Friend makes your heart happy, and your Best Friend feels the same way about you.

A Friend Likes to Play With You

Your Best Friend loves to play with you. And God's playground is the whole world!

You can play hide-and-seek with God. Look for God in the things you see outdoors. If you find a bird's nest, think about how God is like a mother bird. What about a sparkly rock or a snake skin—do those remind you of God in any way?

Whenever you enjoy yourself, God enjoys you too. When you ride your bike so fast you can feel the wind in your hair, God is riding with you. You can't see God—just as you can't see the wind. But God is there, having fun with you.

A Friend Is Fun to Get to Know

As you get to know a friend better, you find out all kinds of amazing things. You can get to know your Friend God better by looking at all the wonderful things God has made and done.

Look at the patterns on a butterfly wing. God is an artist! Think about how dolphins are able to "talk" to each other under water. God is a genius! God controls all the stars and planets in all the galaxies in the whole universe. God is very powerful!

God—your Best Friend—is an Incredible Genius, Mastermind, Amazing Brainiac, Awesome Power, Superhero, Master of the Universe! What a great Friend to have!

God Is No Ordinary Friend

We can't see or hear God the way we can visit and talk with a regular friend. But we can "sense" God—when we look, listen, and feel God's love in our lives.

You can see God's love in the beauty of clouds melting into a pretty sunset. You can smell and taste God's love in the yummy-ness of a chocolate chip cookie. You can touch God's love in the warmth of a grandparent's hug. You can hear God's love in music that wraps itself around your heart.

A Friend Is Always There for You

One of the greatest things about your Best Friend is that God is everywhere!

You can take God to camp with you so you won't get homesick. God can be with you at all your classes in school. You can send God into your closet at night to check for monsters.

If you're not going to see one of your parents for a while, God is there to hold you and take care of you. When you dance with all your heart in your recital, God is there to cheer you on, beaming with pride.

God is closer to you than your own heartbeat... every minute of every day.

Friends Stay in Touch

You can connect with God anytime, anywhere. It's like talking on a wireless phone—except there's no limit on the minutes you can talk, and it's free!

God always has time to listen to you. You can tell God about your day or about something exciting coming up. You can tell God if you're mad or sad or scared. You can tell God whatever is on your mind, and God will understand.

God will answer you, too—not by leaving a message on your answering machine, but by speaking to your heart.

A Friend Helps You

Call on God if you need anything. You can ask your Friend to help you do better in math—or be brave enough to go down the big water slide. When you have to do anything hard, God can help you to find the power inside you.

God often helps in surprising ways. Maybe a new idea about how to solve a problem will just pop into your head. Or maybe God will have another person help you—like if your sister helps you look for your lost library book.

Sometimes God just hugs your heart and makes you feel better!

You Help Your Friend

God is so nice to us, it makes us want to be nice to other people. And God needs our help to make the world a better place.

You can be God's eyes to see when a classmate needs help carrying her lunch tray. You can be God's ears to listen when a friend is upset. You can be God's voice to speak up for someone who is afraid. You can be God's hands to share with a person who doesn't have as much as you.

Going to a Friend's Party

It's so much fun to go to a party at a friend's house! There are often special decorations, food and drinks. There may be gifts and games, candles and singing. We get to meet our friend's family and maybe even hear some favorite family stories.

When our parents take us to a worship service, it's like going to a party at God's house. The people around us are God's family. There are candles, flowers, or other special decorations. We often eat, drink, sing, and pray. We listen to stories about God from the holy books of our faith. And we give God the gift of our hearts.

When a Friend Seems Far Away

Sometimes God can seem far away. If your cat gets hit by a car, or your grandpa is very sick, it might seem like God doesn't care.

You may feel sad and alone. You might even be mad at God, but that's okay. It's normal to feel mad when something in your life is all messed up.

Not even the smartest people in the world understand why bad things happen sometimes. We do know that when we are sad, God is sad too. God holds us the closest when we hurt the most.

A Friend Forgives

Sometimes we do things that hurt our Best Friend. If you tease your little brother, that hurts God, because God loves your little brother too.

Tell your little brother you're sorry. If you messed up something that belongs to him, try to fix it or get him a new one.

Tell God you're sorry, too. God will always forgive you and love you—no matter what!

Best Friends Forever

Each one of us has a special spark of "God-ness" inside us. This spark makes us want to be close to God and to be like God.

When you are kind to others, you are acting out of the "God-ness" of your heart. When you enjoy food, friends, and fun at a picnic, you are enjoying the "God-ness" of creation.

Remember: Right beside you, deep inside you, all around you, God surrounds you. God is always with you—your Best Friend, forever and ever without end!

Lisa O. Engelhardt is the editorial director for product development at Abbey Press. She is the author of ten books, including the Elf-help Book for Kids: *Right and Wrong and Being Strong*. She and her husband and three children live in Lawrenceburg, Indiana.

R. W. Alley is the illustrator for the popular Abbey Press adult series of Elf-help books, as well as an illustrator and writer of children's books. He lives in Barrington, Rhode Island, with his wife, daughter, and son.